# Farmer Skiboo Stories

## Martin Waddell

Illustrated by
**Julie Fletcher**

OXFORD
UNIVERSITY PRESS

# OXFORD
UNIVERSITY PRESS

Great Clarendon Street, Oxford OX2 6DP

Oxford University Press is a department of the University of Oxford.
It furthers the University's objective of excellence in research, scholarship,
and education by publishing worldwide in

Oxford  New York

Auckland  Bangkok  Buenos Aires  Cape Town  Chennai
Dar es Salaam  Delhi  Hong Kong  Istanbul  Karachi  Kolkata
Kuala Lumpur  Madrid  Melbourne  Mexico City  Mumbai  Nairobi
São Paulo  Shanghai  Singapore  Taipei  Tokyo  Toronto

with an associated company in Berlin

Oxford is a registered trade mark of Oxford University Press
in the UK and in certain other countries

British Library Cataloguing in Publication Data

Data available

ISBN 0 19 919479 3

1 3 5 7 9 10 8 6 4 2

Guided Reading Pack (6 of the same title):  ISBN 0 19 919556 0
Mixed Pack (1 of 6 different titles):  ISBN 0 19 919483 1
Class Pack (6 copies of 6 titles):  ISBN 0 19 919484 X

Printed in Hong Kong

# Contents

# Cock-a-doodle-doo

It was midnight,
and the farmyard was still.
The full moon rose over the hill.
It flooded the farm with its light.

"I'll play a trick on Farmer Skiboo,"
thought Barn Owl.

He went, *"Too-wit-too-woooo,"* very softly.
It was just loud enough to waken the
Silly Old Rooster.

"What's this?" thought the Silly Old Rooster. "I'm awake. It must be dawn."

He went, *"Cock-a-doodle-doo,"* to wake up the rest of the farm.

**Cock-a-doodle-doo**

The cows in the field heard
the Silly Old Rooster calling.
They thought it must be morning.

"It's milking time," thought the cows.
"There goes the Rooster!"

And they went, "*Moo-moo-moo-mooo,*"
calling for someone to milk them.

***Cock-a-doodle-doo***
***Moo-moo-moo-mooo***

7

Brown Hen was asleep in the hedge.
The noise wakened her.

"There goes the Rooster.
It must be time for my egg," she said.

She laid one at once.
And she went, *"Cluck-cluck-cluck-cluck,"*
because she was so pleased with
the egg she had laid.

*Cock-a-doodle-doo*
*Moo-moo-moo-mooo*
*Cluck-cluck-cluck-cluck*

The ducks and the ducklings were down by the pond.

"He's done it again. That Silly Old Rooster has wakened Brown Hen!" they decided. "It must be time for our swim."

They all waddled in for their swim.

And the ducks and ducklings went
*"Quack-quack-quack-quack,"*
the way all ducks do,
when the water is cold in the morning.

*Cock-a-doodle-doo*
*Moo-moo-moo-mooo*
*Cluck-cluck-cluck-cluck*
*Quack-quack-quack-quack*

10

Faithful Dog Tom was asleep
in the farmer's armchair.
He was too old to sleep out of doors.
    "There goes the Silly Old Rooster.
It must be get-up-and-do time
for the farmer and me!" he thought.

Faithful Dog Tom padded upstairs.
He pushed open the door of the
farmer's bedroom.

And he barked,
*"Bow-wow-wow-woooooo,"*
to wake up Farmer Skiboo.

*Cock-a-doodle-doo*
*Moo-moo-moo-mooo*
*Cluck-cluck-cluck-cluck*
*Quack-quack-quack-quack*
*Bow-wow-wow-woooooo*

Farmer Skiboo was in bed.
The barking woke him up.
   He climbed out of bed
without waking Mrs Skiboo.
He yawned and scratched.
He put on his boots and his hat.
He pulled back the curtains
to let in the light of the morning.

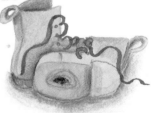

Farmer Skiboo saw the moon
shining bright.

"*OO-OO-OO-OO-OOOH!*"
moaned Farmer Skiboo.

*Cock-a-doodle-doo*
*Moo-moo-moo-mooo*
*Cluck-cluck-cluck-cluck*
*Quack-quack-quack-quack*
*Bow-wow-wow-woooooo*
*OO-OO-OO-OO-OOOH!*

The moon shone down on
   the Silly Old Rooster crowing,
   the cows who were mooing,
   Brown Hen and her egg,
   the cold ducks who swam on the pond,
   Faithful Dog Tom,
   and Farmer Skiboo.
   *"STOP THAT NOISE!*
*GET BACK TO BED!"* yelled Farmer Skiboo.
He was dancing and prancing with rage.

He took off his boot
and chucked it at the Silly Old Rooster.
*CRASH-BANG-SMACK-WALLOP-YAROOO!*

*Cock-a-doodle-doo*
*Moo-moo-moo-mooo*
*Cluck-cluck-cluck-cluck*
*Bow-wow-wow-woooooo*
*OO-OO-OO-OO-OOOH!*
*STOP-THAT-NOISE!*
*GET-BACK-TO-BED!*
*CRASH-BANG-SMACK-WALLOP-*
*YAROOO!*

All the noise stopped at once.

The farmyard was peaceful and quiet
and still. The animals went back to sleep.

The only sound was the squeak
of the springs as Farmer Skiboo
climbed into bed.

And then …
Someone called,
*"Too-wit-too-woooo,"* very softly.
It was just loud enough to waken the
Silly Old Rooster and …

*Cock-a-doodle-doo*
*Moo-moo-moo-mooo*
*Cluck-cluck-cluck-cluck*
*Quack-quack-quack-quack*
*Bow-wow-wow-woooooo*
*OO-OO-OO-OO-OOOH!*
*STOP-THAT-NOISE!*
*GET-BACK-TO-BED!*
*CRASH-BANG-SMACK-WALLOP-*
*YAROOOOOO!*

# Four Fools in a Field

## Chapter 1
# A Problem for Charlie

Farmer Skiboo called Charlie to help with
the bull.

Charlie looked at the bull.

The bull looked at Charlie.

The bull didn't think much of Charlie.

"Get the bull out of this field, Charlie,"
said Farmer Skiboo. "But don't wreck
my hedge when you do it!"

"Right!" said Charlie.

Charlie looked at the bull and the hedge.
The hedge was quite small.
The bull was a whole lot of bull.

How could Charlie
get the bull over the hedge?
He didn't know.

"Well, here goes, I suppose!"
Charlie said.

He crawled in under the bull.

The bull looked in under himself.

He saw Charlie there …

He still didn't think much
of Charlie.

Charlie tried to stand up.

He had the bull on his back.

He was trying to lift the bull over the hedge.

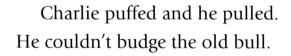

Charlie puffed and he pulled.
He couldn't budge the old bull.

"Ned!" Charlie said. "Give me a hand with this bull."

Ned took one end of the bull.

Charlie stood at the other.

They puffed and they pulled.

They still couldn't budge the old bull.

"Send for Bert and Sid," Ned told Charlie.

Bert and Sid came, and they each took
a leg of the bull.

"ONE, TWO, THREE, LIFT."

And they puffed and they pulled,
but they couldn't budge that old bull.

# Chapter 2
## Stuck Charlie!

They sat down to think.

The four fools looked at the bull.

The bull looked at the fools.

The bull didn't think much of the fools.

"We could dig a bull tunnel, under the hedge," Charlie said.

Nobody wanted to dig.

"We're stuck with that bull!" Charlie said.

## Chapter *3*

# *Small Anne to the Rescue*

Along came Farmer Skiboo's daughter, Small Anne.

"I know how to do it!" she said.

Small Anne opened the gate.

She LED the bull out of the field, without touching the hedge.

She closed the gate.

She patted the bull on the head.

Then Small Anne walked away whistling.

Ned, Bert, and Sid beamed at the bull.
But Charlie stood scratching his head.

"What if Farmer Skiboo wants that
bull BACK in the field?" Charlie said.
"How can we put the bull back without
busting the hedge?"

"I dunno ..." sighed Ned.

"Me neither!"
sobbed Bert.

"Forget it!" said Sid.

Then ...
"GOT IT!" Charlie said.
"If he wants the bull back
in the field, we just send
for Small Anne."
And that's what they did.

# About the author

I have been trying to get Farmer Skiboo into a story for ages. Why? Because I like the way the words work together. A farmer with a name like "Skiboo" sounded interesting to work on. So I needed a farm story. Skiboo... and cock-a-doodle-doo... do you see what I mean about the sound of the words?

The best stories often begin that way.